To Daniele, Drew and Suz

Copyright © 2004 Craig Frazier.
All rights reserved.

Typeset in Century Schoolbook.
The illustrations in this book are hand-drawn
and colored on the computer.
Manufactured in Hong Kong.

Library of Congress Cataloging-in-Publication Data
Frazier, Craig, 1955-
    Stanley goes for a drive / by Craig Frazier.
        p. cm.
  Summary: Stanley goes for a drive on a hot day in the countryside.
    ISBN 0-8118-4429-3
    [1. Country life—Fiction. 2. Heat—Fiction.] I. Title.
    PZ7.F869St 2004
    [E]—dc22
  2003021243

Distributed in Canada by Raincoast Books
9050 Shaughnessy Street, Vancouver, British Columbia V6P 6E5

10 9 8 7 6 5 4 3 2 1

Chronicle Books LLC
85 Second Street, San Francisco, California 94105

www.chroniclekids.com

STANLEY

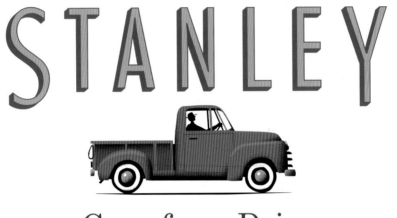

Goes for a Drive

Craig Frazier

chronicle books·san francisco

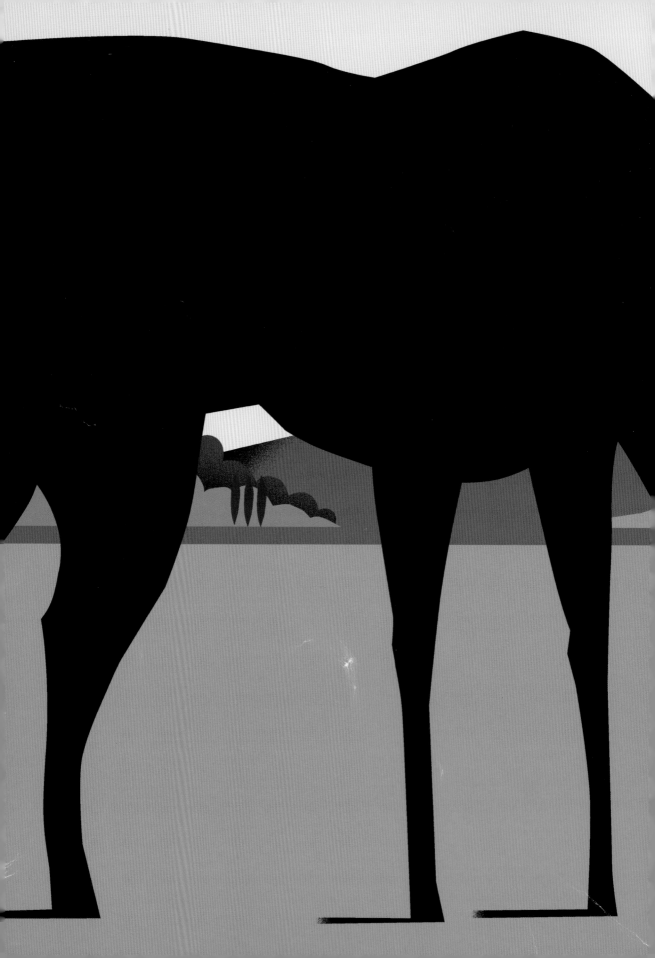

Stanley set out on a drive
with little on his mind.

Clouds of dust billowed from the wheels
of Stanley's old pickup as he motored
down the country road.

There wasn't a cloud in the sky, just the baking hot sun. The barn roof was hot enough to fry an egg. The pond was so dry that it couldn't even make a reflection.

Thunder, the black horse,
whinnied as Stanley drove by.

Stanley passed a herd of cows.

Suddenly, Stanley slammed on the brakes.

Stanley had an idea.

As Stanley milked the spotted cow, something very strange began to happen.

And it got even stranger.

The sky darkened and
Stanley's clouds began to pour.

When the rain stopped,
everything had changed.

Bright, puffy clouds cast their cool shadows. The pond was full once again. The cows were eating the tall, green grass. Stanley turned his truck around...

...and headed home.

Mooo.